For Roel, because I'm so glad that you are who you are — Marlise

Winner of the Inclusive Works award for children's stories.

First published in Belgium and Holland by Clavis Uitgeverij, Hasselt – Amsterdam, 2013
Copyright © 2013, Clavis Uitgeverij

English translation from the Dutch by Clavis Publishing Inc. New York
Copyright © 2015 for the English language edition:
Clavis Publishing Inc. New York

Visit us on the web at www.clavisbooks.com

Princess Nina written by Marlise Achterbergh
and illustrated by Iris Compiet
Original title: *Prinses Nina*
Translated from the Dutch by Clavis Publishing

ISBN 978-1-60537-222-8

This book was printed in March 2015 at Proost Industries NV,
Everdongenlaan 23, 2300 Turnhout, Belgium

First Edition
10 9 8 7 6 5 4 3 2 1

Clavis Publishing supports the First Amendment and celebrates the right to read

Princess Nina

Marlise Achterbergh & Iris Compiet

Clavis
NEW YORK

Once upon a time there was an extraordinary
princess named *Princess Feminina*,
but everyone called her *Nina*.
Princess *Nina* was smart, curious,
sweet, and **spunky**.

Her clothes were always
covered in stains, and
the cook's naughty jokes
made her giggle.
She loved the color red
and riding horseback.
She was also fond
of cooking and baked
cakes so big that
they almost didn't fit
in the royal oven.

One day the king and queen decided it was time they found
a prince for *Princess Nina*. But the princess disagreed.
She yelled that she didn't want a prince. "Look at Princess Fatima,
Princess Ishiko and Princess Noortje," her surprised parents replied.
"They are all going to marry princes. That's how it should be."
But *Princess Nina* wouldn't talk about it!
She ran to her room in a fury. "It'll pass," the queen said
and she decided to invite a few princes to visit anyway.

The first prince who came to visit was
Prince Guozhi. He was tall and strong and brought
fireworks in more than a hundred colors.
Princess Nina loved the show and invited
the prince to go **riding** with her.

When *Princess Nina* and *Prince Guozhi* raced, he lost
three times in a row – even when the princess was riding
her horse backwards! So he decided they were a bad match.

The next prince who came by was *Prince Esteban*.
He knew the names of all the countries in the world
and had a talent for math, solving riddles, and thinking long and hard.
Princess Nina invited him to go **swimming** in the river.

But *Prince Esteban* thought the water was **too cold**, the current was **too strong**, and the ground was **too dirty**. Besides, he had forgotten to bring his swimming trunks. When *Princess Nina* **playfully splashed water on him**, he got angry and **stormed off.**

The next day *Prince Gauthier* came to visit.
Princess Nina baked him a cake,
but **he didn't like the way she whipped the cream.**

He refused a **fencing match** because he said it wasn't a sport for girls. Then he told her she should comb her hair. *Princess Nina* sent him **home.**

Prince Azim arrived on a white horse.
He brought diamonds, camels, and one
hundred red roses for *Princess Nina*.
He held the door for her like a gentleman,
he was a good listener and **his eyes were
beautiful.** His jokes made *Princess Nina*
laugh all day long. *Prince Azim* also told dreamy
stories about the desert. He wore spicy cologne,
and made the best mint tea she had ever tasted.
After he serenaded her underneath her window,
he asked *Princess Nina* to marry him.
The king and queen looked out from their turret room,
filled with hope — **but** *Princess Nina* **said no.**

Princess Nina's parents didn't know what to do. They asked some of
their royal friends for advice and invited them to visit. One of the
royal couples accepted the invitation and brought their daughter,
Princess Melowo, with them.

Princess Melowo had many talents: she spoke seven languages, had a lovely singing voice, and built castles all by herself. When *Princess Nina* saw her, she noticed the stains on her own dress. Her **cheeks flushed**, and she didn't know what to say. For the **first time** in her life, *Princess Nina* **was shy.**

That night *Princess Nina* couldn't sleep. She thought
about *Princess Melowo*: the way she walked and moved
her hands, the stories she told, the sound of her voice.
Princess Nina felt a tickle in her belly.

The next day *Princess Melowo* taught
Princess Nina how to make banana chips.
When *Princess Melowo* got close, *Princess Nina*
felt as though **butterflies** were flying around in
her tummy. The kitchen smelled wonderful all day
long, and the cook asked for at least a dozen recipes.

The days flew by.
Princess Nina was so **happy**
she'd met *Princess Melowo.*
They spent every day together
doing interesting things.
But what *Princess Nina* enjoyed the most was
when they sat outside and gazed at the stars.
The princesses didn't talk, but just sat and
watched the sky. Sometimes they heard
a cricket or the wind, but most of the time
it was quiet and all they felt was their
warm backs against each other.

When it was time for *Princess Melowo* to pack her bags
and go home, *Princess Nina* felt **very sad**, as if there
were a rock in her stomach. She didn't want *Princess
Melowo* to leave. Luckily *Princess Melowo* had an idea
that made *Princess Nina* **very happy**....

"I would like to marry Princess Melowo," *Princess Nina* told her parents. The king and queen were surprised. They had always thought *Princess Nina* was going to marry a prince. "Do you want to marry *Princess Nina*?" the king asked *Princess Melowo* in a soft voice. "Yes!" *Princess Melowo* yelled. "I love *Princess Nina* more than I love anyone!" "I've noticed that," her mother said, "and that's why I think it is a wonderful idea." "Two queens!" *Princess Melowo's* father called out enthusiastically. "Now, that sounds like fun!" *Princess Nina's* mother said: "I think this choice suits *Princess Nina* very well." Her father nodded. "Hurrah!" the cook yelled. "I'd better start **baking the wedding cake**!"

The kings and queens gave a huge party
to celebrate the marriage of the two princesses.
There were solemn speeches, cheerful music,
a beautiful wedding cake, and the best banana chips
in the whole wide world. And that's how the country
came to have **two queens**:
Queen Feminina and *Queen Melowo*.
The land had never been ruled better,
and everyone lived **happily ever after**.